I_

ANT'S

AWESOME

ADVENTURE

by

Maureen Boon

Illust ted by Tmsson Hollam

GW00579644

Published by Maureen Boon in 2019

ISBN 978-1-9161178-0-8

Cover by Harrison Pigeon

Acknowledgements

I would like to thank all members of my family and friends for their encouragement and support. In particular, my husband Robert, for looking after the dogs when I went to Spain for a week to finish this story and proofreading the final manuscript.

Also, many thanks to Imogen for her illustrations and her patience with all my changes to her drafts.

Chapter 1 Ant is puzzled

Day 1 Tuesday morning

"What are you doing here, boy?" asked the skinny man in the caretaker's overall.

"Looking for Mr. Gimble," Ant replied nervously.

"He's gone. Now get out of here. Pupils aren't allowed in here."

Ant was taken aback. Why wouldn't Mr. Gimble be there? Was he ill? He remembered before the holidays, the last thing Mr. Gimble had said was, "See you in September, Ant. Have a good holiday."

His mind flashed back to his first meeting with Mr. Gimble on September 20th last year. It was his third week at big school. It had been a bad day for Ant.

As usual he had done what his mum had suggested. The night before he had sorted his school bag so that his homework was there for maths the next day, his gym kit for P.E. in the afternoon and his lunch card (which Mum had already made sure had credit) was in the front pocket with his bus pass. He put his school uniform and underwear in reverse order on the chair in his bedroom and set his alarm for 7.30 a.m.

"Strange, you might think if you didn't know me," he reflected to himself in the mirror, as he cleaned his teeth, "You might think I am a bit OCD!"

Amy, a friend of his at school, had told him that she had OCD, Obsessive Compulsive Disorder. She was always worried about germs and things being clean and everything in the right place. She made him promise not to tell anyone.

He chuckled at his reflection, because he was, of course, quite the opposite. Ant had been diagnosed with dyspraxia when he was still at primary school and this nightly routine was his way of helping him to cope with secondary school. Generally, he wasn't very well coordinated, had problems with buttons and laces and organizing himself for school.

He looked at the *Velcro* fastening on his tie, he knew that was OK because the school rule was that ties had to be fixed that way, since two years ago, when his cousin, Paul had been 'peanutted'. He sighed thinking about Paul, who had had a red mark around his neck for nearly a week. The bully, who had found it funny to tighten Paul's tie like that, had been suspended from school and the head had changed the rules about ties right away. "Thank goodness!" he thought to himself.

His *Velcro* shoes were all right because lots of people had *Velcro* fastening shoes these days, he was glad to say. What was not OK were the *Velcro* fastenings on his shirt. He sighed, he had told Mum that it was better to end up with his shirt fastened any old how, than to have *Velcro* fastenings. And the shoes - another bone of contention with Mum – were marked 'R' for right and 'L' for left in large letters on the inside for everyone to see in the changing room.

Ant groaned and went to bed. The next morning, thanks to Mum hassling him, he was on the bus in time, looking neat and tidy.

Everything went well until P.E. in the afternoon. It was hockey, a team game. First of all, Mr. Bowley, the teacher picked Matt and Dan to choose their teams – of course he *would* pick them because they were the best players. Ant stood there whilst they chose first one person and then another. In the end, there were only two of them left, him and his mate Hal. Then

Matt picked by Hal, followed by Dan, who said "Ant," with a grimace.

He spent the whole game near the side of the pitch, following the ball up and down and never managing to connect with it once. His team lost. He wandered off the pitch as soon as he could to the changing room and amazingly found he was first there.

With a sign of relief, he started the long ordeal of getting changed. He was doing up his shirt when Bazza and Macca charged in.

"It's the *Velcro* boy," laughed Bazza, "I'll give you a hand!" He grabbed Ant's shirt and fastened it up so that it looked ridiculous, the equivalent of two buttons out.

"Ha, ha," chortled Macca, "Let's get your shoes on the right feet."

The two of them proceeded to push the 'R' shoe on the left foot and the 'L' shoe on the right foot.

The rest of the class then came in the changing room, chatting and laughing. Then they saw Ant and started laughing even louder – all except his mate Hal, who sank into the coat hooks behind the jumpers and trousers, trying to disappear.

In came Mr. Bowley. "Quiet!" he shouted, "What's going on here! Anthony Collins, why are you playing the fool? Sort yourself out! Parsons and MacLean, calm down."

Ant groaned inwardly, "It's not my fault Mr. Bowley, it was them!" he protested.

"Stop making excuses. You're always in the middle of it, Collins. All of you, get changed and go to your next lesson or I'll put you *all* in detention."

Everyone went quiet and finished getting changed. Ant was last out, trying to tidy himself up and as he left the sports hall. Macca and Bazza were waiting outside.

"Better get a move on, Collins!" shouted Macca, whilst Bazza strategically aimed a kick at his backside sending him stumbling up the path. They ran past him jeering and laughing, "Watch out *Velcro* boy! Get your shoes on right or you might fall over!"

Ant sank down on the ground behind the sports hall and cried. What could he do? People were so unkind and cruel. Where was Hal? He knew that Hal was just as scared of incurring the wrath of people like Macca and Bazza as he was.

He felt a hand on his shoulder and shrank into himself. Had they come back?

He looked up and saw a kindly man smiling down at him.

"Lad," he said, "I saw what those boys were up to. Come with me and have a cup of tea."

The man in a long khaki coat held out his hand and helped him up. He patted him on the back. "It's OK, lad. You'll be fine."

Ant followed him as they went through a door in a small building next to the sports hall and down a rickety stair. At the bottom the man turned left through a door marked, 'Mr. Gimble, Caretaker'.

"Sit down here lad," said Mr. Gimble motioning to an old battered armchair with a squashy yellow patterned cushion on it.

Ant sat down and relaxed. He felt safe at last.

"Do you take milk and sugar?" asked Mr. Gimble, switching the kettle on and taking two mugs out of the cupboard over the sink.

"Yes please, two sugars," muttered Ant quietly.

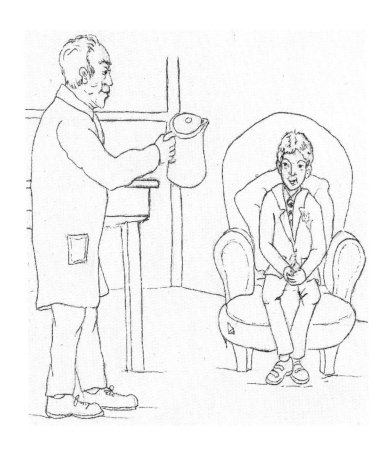

Ant and Mr. Gimble have a cup
of tea.

Ant sat down and relaxed. He felt safe at last.

"Do you take milk and sugar?" asked Mr. Gimble, switching the kettle on and taking two mugs out of the cupboard over the sink.

"Yes please, two sugars," muttered Ant quietly.

That was the first time. They drank their tea in a companionable silence. Then Mr. Gimble said, "You'd better be going now, lad, so you don't miss your next lesson. If anyone asks where you were this lesson, say you felt a bit peculiar after games and had to go to the toilet."

Ant nodded and started to climb the stairs muttering a 'thank you' to Mr. Gimble.

"Anytime you feel you need a safe place and a cuppa, just pop in," said Mr. Gimble as Ant went out through the door.

Over the school year, Ant had popped in to see Mr. Gimble many times and usually had a cup of tea. After the first quiet visit, they now always had what Mr. Gimble called 'a good natter'. Ant found out that Mr. Gimble liked fishing and had a rowing boat by the quayside and Ant told him that he belonged to the local Sea Scouts. He told Mr. Gimble that he had never been any good at sports. He had gone for special exercise and swimming classes with the local physiotherapy services and learnt to swim.

They were really patient and taught him well. Then, Maggie, his physio, suggested to Mum and Dad, that it might be a good idea to take up sailing as a hobby, as he was such a good swimmer. This was a brilliant idea because his dad had a little sailing boat. Later when he was ten and a half, he joined the Sea Scouts and was learning how to sail on his own, rather than just crewing for Dad. He told Mr. Gimble that the Sea Scouts were great and that he actually had shown them he was quite a good sailor. The other boys were friendly too, no bullying there.

Ant and Mr. Gimble also discovered that they both had a passion for Agatha Christie programmes on TV; Poirot was Ant's favourite, but Mr. Gimble had a soft spot for Miss Marple. They both had taken a fancy to 'Murder in Paradise' and discussed the cases each week.

Suddenly Ant came back to the present with a jump. The thin man was staring at him in exasperation. "Wake up boy. I said you're not allowed in here. Get out!"

Ant stared at him in puzzlement. "What d'you mean, Mr. Gimble's gone?" he blurted out.

The skinny man looked irritated, "He's left. I'm the new caretaker and I'm telling you to leave. This area is out of bounds."

He stared at Ant and looked towards the steps which led up to the door.

"Go!" he said, sounding like he was getting to the end of his tether, "Go, or I'll report you to your form teacher!"

Ant didn't understand what was going on. Where was Mr. Gimble? Where had he gone? Why had he left? How could he find out what had happened to him? His mind was going around in circles.

Then he had a brainwave, he thought of Mr. Gimble's neighbour. He would go round there with Hal and ask the neighbour. Mr. Gimble can't have died – they would have said something in assembly. Usually, they were told when a member of staff was leaving and would give them a clap and sometimes three cheers. No one had said anything at the end of term about Mr. Gimble.

Yes, he would go and find Hal and they would go and have a look round the outside of Mr. Gimble's house after school to try and find out what had happened. He suddenly felt a bit more positive because then they would know what had occurred and usually, hopefully, the real thing would not be as bad as what you might have imagined. Fingers crossed!

Chapter 2 Ant visits Mr. Gimble's house

Day 1 Tuesday afternoon

"But Ant," Hal said, as they walked through the school gate, "Say if Mr. Gimble's there. He'll think we're mad."

"No, he won't, he'll give us a cup of tea and a chocolate biscuit and ask us how we're getting on, just like he always does."

"I suppose," pondered Hal, "But say if we find his body and no one knew he had died."

"Don't be daft, Hal. If he just hadn't turned up to school after the holidays, then someone would have gone round to see where he was. Anyway, he usually works during the holidays and so someone would have found out if he'd gone missing."

They were nearly there because Mr. Gimble's house was quite close to the school. He lived near Hal's nan and they had often seen him in his garden when they went to see her last year. Hal's mum was always sending him round with things for her, like cakes and biscuits. Mr. Gimble had always waved and shouted, "Hi guys, how are you doing?"

They stood outside the house. The grass was long; that was odd. The plants in the pot outside his door looked dry and wilted, as if they hadn't been watered for a while. Mr. Gimble had always had the neatest garden in the close. They slowly walked round the back, opening the side gate which creaked ominously. The back was the same.

The plants in the pot outside
the door were dry and wilted.

No one had cut the grass or weeded the flower beds for a few weeks.

"He's not here," said Hal. Ant nodded, thinking that Hal hadn't needed to say that, it was obvious. He stood on tiptoes and looked through the kitchen window. There were plates stacked on the draining board which had been washed but not put away. They moved to the next window and saw there were newspapers stacked on the coffee table and an empty mug stood next to them.

"Well, he's not moved house that's for sure," commented Ant.

"Maybe he's upstairs, you know ... dead," said Hal looking worried.

"No, I told you before, someone from school would have found out if it was that. Let's go and knock on next door and ask if they've seen him."

Hal made a face, "The man next door is a bit grumpy. He shouted at me when I accidently kicked a ball over Nan's fence."

Ant gritted his teeth, "I'll ask," he said bravely, not feeling that way at all, but hiding it from Hal.

He rang the doorbell.

The man opened the door and looked down at them. He looked more than mildly irritated at having to answer the door. "Yes? What do you two want?"

"We're looking for Mr. Gimble from Meadowfield School. Do you know where he is?"

"He's gone. Left at the end of July. Went in a taxi. He was here one day and gone the next."

"Where has he gone?" uttered Ant, but it was too late, the man had shut the door in their faces.

"Let's see if Nan knows," offered Hal helpfully.

"Why didn't you think of that before?" said Ant with a sigh.

Nan gave them some juice and biscuits and asked Hal how his mum and sister were.

The conversation went on and on. In the end Ant jumped in when she paused for breath, "Mrs. Green, do you know where Mr. Gimble's gone?"

She turned to him and smiled, "Why, Australia of course. When he was getting in the taxi, I asked him and he said, 'Australia, to see my sister, I've not seen her for 20 years.' "

"Was it a surprise?" Ant asked.

"Well, you could've knocked me down with a feather! A couple of weeks before he was telling me he was planning a weekend in Bournemouth and then he was gone – to Australia. He told me he had won an airline ticket and decided to go. He told the headmaster he would be away for the term. Back after Christmas."

"He won an airline ticket? Why couldn't he leave it until later when it's summer in Australia?" Ant was puzzled as he knew that Australian seasons were the opposite of those in the U.K.

"It was a condition of his ticket," said Mrs. Green, "He had to go within a week. Luckily one of the teachers knew someone who was looking for a temporary job as a caretaker."

"Mr. Brownlees wasn't acting like he was temporary," thought Ant to himself. Ant had noticed as he was leaving the caretaker's office, that Mr. Brownlees had already put his name up on the door.

It was very strange and Ant was sure that something odd was going on.

When they left Mrs. Green, Ant told Hal that he was going to investigate and look round the caretaker's office when he wasn't there.

"But how are you going to do that, Ant," asked Hal, "He's always hanging around his office."

"Yes, but I know that he meets the headmaster once a week to talk about jobs which need doing, you know like painting, cutting the grass, putting lines on the football pitch – that sort of thing. Mr.

Gimble always went to see the head on Wednesday afternoons at 1 o' clock."

"But if you get caught poking around in his office you could get suspended," Hal looked worried.

"I won't get caught," said Ant, "If someone sees me, I'll tell them I was taking something to 'Lost Property'."

"Right," nodded Hal, "Of course, 'Lost Property' is in the caretaker's office. But what about lessons, you'll miss the extra English class we go to. What are you going to say?"

"I'll see the school nurse at lunchtime and say I'm sick. No one will know."

"But she'll phone your mum if you're sick."

"Oh, yes. You're right. Well, I'll just not turn up and you can say I've gone home sick."

Hal looked at him dubiously, "What if *I* get found out?"

"Just tell them that I told you I was sick."

Hal nodded reluctantly.

Chapter 3 Ant makes a discovery

Day 2 Wednesday

Ant was waiting near the steps down to the caretaker's office at 12.45 the next day. He had hidden himself round the corner by the sports hall and peeped round to see Mr. Brownlees leaving at 12.50. He breathed a sigh of relief as the thin man disappeared out of sight through a door into the main school. Ant quickly went down the stairs to the caretaker's office. It looked a bit different from when Mr. Gimble was there. Mr. Brownlees had installed a new, office-type chair and a new computer was on the desk. The teapot had gone and in its place was a new coffee machine that looked like something out of a sci-fi film.

Ant went into the inner part of the room where the supplies were kept and mooched around. He checked the drawers and cupboards – washing up liquid, floor cleaner, white paint, cloths, scrubbing brushes. All was what you would expect. He sighed and perched on a pair of folding steps. Maybe Hal was right, perhaps he was paranoid and there was nothing to discover. Next, he looked in a big walk-in cupboard, but it was full of brooms, buckets and mops. Then he looked round the outer room again. Underneath the workbench was a big plastic box with a clip-on lid. He knelt down and pulled the box, but it wouldn't move. It was very heavy.

The box was full of ornaments
and jewels!

Ant crawled under the workbench and levered the lid off. His mouth dropped open in surprise; he could hardly believe what he was seeing. The box was full of ornaments and jewels which looked very ornate and old. He picked up a gold ring with a huge red jewel on it and gasped in amazement.

Then he heard the outside door open and footsteps at the top of the stairs. He rammed the ring in his pocket. He pushed the lid back on the box and retreated into the broom cupboard as fast as he could. He just made it as he saw feet coming down the stairs and gently pulled the door behind him. He couldn't believe he had moved so quickly and quietly. "It must be fear," he reflected to himself, "How I didn't trip up is amazing." He held his breath and heard the sound of someone moving around the room.

There was a crack in the door and Ant peered through to see Mr. Brownlees pick up a blue folder from his workbench and turn to leave. Then he stopped and seemed to be looking straight at him. Ant froze. Then Mr. Brownlees turned, knelt down and opened the box under the workbench. Ant realized, with relief, that Mr. Brownlees could not see him but was just checking his hoard.

At last, Mr. Brownlees got up and left, with his forgotten folder, to go back to the headmaster's office.

Ant finally let his breath out and started breathing normally again as he heard the outside door shut. He realized that his heart was pounding and his legs were shaking. He counted to 30, then crept up the stairs and cautiously opened the door. There was no sign of Mr. Brownlees, Ant sneaked out and went to the school gate via the sports hall and round the rugby pitch, so that he did not have to go in the main building again.

He kept looking behind himself all the way home and didn't relax until he was in his bedroom. He put his hand in his pocket and pulled the ring out. It was amazing – gold and probably a ruby. It looked really old. What was Mr. Brownlees up to?

Chapter 4 Ant makes plans

Day 2 Wednesday evening

Hal came round after his tea, at about 6 o'clock, to see how Ant had got on. They went up to Ant's bedroom. Ant showed Hal the ring.

"Wha-a-a-t!" Hal exclaimed, "I don't believe it! A ring!"

"Shhh," whispered Ant, "Don't let Mum and Dad hear."

"But it looks old and it must be worth a lot of money," mused Hal, "What's that red stone, is it a real jewel?"

"I think it might be a ruby," said Ant, "And there were lots more things, all old."

"I don't believe it! A ring!" Hal
exclaimed.

"There was a lot of jewellery – rings, necklaces, bracelets, brooches and ornaments too. They all looked like they were made of gold and there were lots of jewels – red, blue, green, white …"

"Diamonds!" hissed Hal excitedly.

"Maybe," nodded Ant, "Mr. Brownlees had them all in a really big plastic crate under the workbench."

"But what does it mean? Where did they come from? Has it got something to do with Mr. Gimble going to Australia?"

Ant shook his head, "I don't think it can have anything to do with Mr. Gimble. Your Nan said he had won a ticket to Australia. He was just lucky. I can't wait to tell him about this when he comes back after Christmas."

"But where did Mr. Brownlees get the jewellery from? Do you think he stole them?"

"I don't know," answered Ant, "They *might* belong to him. I know he's a grumpy man but just because he's got these jewels, it doesn't make him a criminal. Maybe he's just storing the jewels there because it's safer in school than at his house."

"But, Ant, say if he finds out the ring is missing, he'll report it to the police."

"Well if he does, then we will know he's legit and I'll leave the ring near his door for him to find. But if he doesn't, then we'll know that he's up to something dodgy."

Ant looked at the ring again, turning it around and holding it up to the light.

"I know it looks valuable, but it might not be. It might be – you know – artificial for some play or acting group..." Ant paused and knitted his brows in thought.

"I know, I'll show Grandad. He'll know if it's real or not. I'll tell him I found it on the pavement and ask him what he thinks. We'll go and see him after school tomorrow."

Chapter 5 Ant consults Grandad

Day 3, Thursday afternoon

The next day after school Ant and Hal went over to Ant's grandad's. They took his favourite biscuits with them – custard creams.

"Oh, you shouldn't have done that, Ant! It's great just to see you and have a chat," said Grandad.

'I wanted to ask you for some advice,' said Ant hesitantly.

"Advice? Well fire away, lad. I'll do what I can," replied Grandad looking intrigued.

"Well it's this," Ant took the ring out of his pocket, "I found it on the pavement and I wondered if I should take to the Police Station."

"My, oh, my, that looks valuable," Grandad held the ring up to the window and examined it, "I'm pretty sure it's a ruby and set in gold. It looks very old."

"But what should I do with it?" asked Ant.

"Take it to the Police Station, as you said. I believe if it's not claimed that you might be allowed to keep it."

"Really!" interjected Hal, "That's amazing!"

"That looks valuable," said
Grandad.

"I'm not one hundred per cent sure," Grandad said quickly, "You need to ask the police when you take it in."

After a cup of tea and biscuits, they said goodbye to Grandad and started back towards home.

Hal said, "Just think, Ant – you could get money for that ring!"

"I know, Hal – but that's not the point. Where has the jewellery come from? Is Mr. Gimble really in Australia or has Mr. Brownlees imprisoned him somewhere? Is Mr. Gimble still alive?"

"Ant, you are over-reacting. It might be that Mr. Gimble is in Australia, as my nan said, and Mr. Brownlees might own the crate of jewellery."

"You really believe that?" Ant looked at Hal quizzically, "Well I intend to investigate. We'll find out where the school thinks Mr. Gimble is and where Mr. Brownlees came from."

"How do you intend to do that?" Hal looked worried.

"Well, we'll ask Mrs. Martin where he is next time we have extra English. She always seems to know everything about what's happening in school. We can go to the office and look at the staff files as well. Find out which school he was at last and where he lives."

"Oh yes," said Hal making a face, "And we just walk in and ask to look at the files! They're confidential you know. Only the headmaster and maybe his secretary are allowed to look at them."

"I have an idea how we can do it," Ant patted his nose mysteriously, "But first we'll ask Mrs. Martin casually about Mr. Gimble at Extra English tomorrow."

Hal raised his eyebrows and sighed – really Ant was taking this far too seriously.

Chapter 6 Ant investigates

Day 4 Friday morning

Ant and Hal rushed to Extra English after assembly. They wanted to get there early and have a chat with Mrs. Martin, the teaching assistant.

"You've got to do the talking, Ant," said Hal, "I'll just get nervous and forget what to say."

"It's OK, Hal," said Ant seriously, I woke up early this morning and wrote everything down and learnt it off by heart."

"What?"

"Well you know how it is, if I'm under stress then I start stammering and tripping over my words. So, if I memorise it and practice it, then, hopefully, I might get it right." Ant grinned and winked at Hal, "Fingers crossed!"

As they hoped, when they got to the classroom Mrs. Martin was there. Their teacher, Mr. Jenkins, hadn't arrived yet.

"Um, Mrs. Martin ...." started Ant, "I was just wondering, have you seen Mr. Gimble lately? I was going to ask him about whether my tie, which I lost last term, was in 'Lost Property'?"

"No, I haven't, but I heard a rumour he's gone to Australia. We've got a temporary caretaker now, Mr. Brownlees. Have you seen him?"

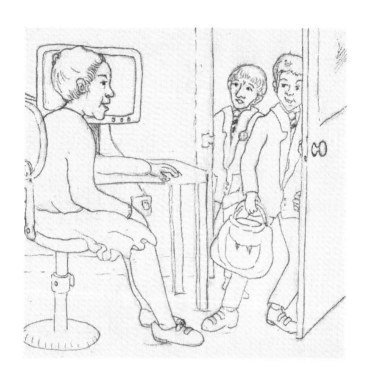

"I heard a rumour that Mr.
Gimble had gone to Australia,"
said Mrs. Martin.

"Yes, but he's different from Mr. Gimble. He doesn't talk to us, you know, to the pupils much."

"Well, he certainly keeps himself to himself. I can't say I've ever seen him in the staffroom. He knows Mr. Potts, the history teacher, I think. They both used to work at the same school some time ago."

At that moment, Mr. Jenkins, walked in at great speed.

"Right everyone, settle down. Sorry I'm late. Had to go to the office to make a phone call. Let's have a look at those spellings we did last time."

Hal and Ant sat down at the big table with the four other pupils. They liked Mr.

Jenkins. He always explained things well and was funny too – cracking jokes and telling stories. Anyway, it was time for work, but Ant kept thinking about his plan to discover out more about Mr. Brownlees and found it difficult to keep his mind on what he was doing.

"Ah well," he thought to himself ruefully, "I never have been able to multitask."

After the lesson it was break time and Ant explained his plan to Hal.

"This is what we'll do," he looked at Hal intently, speaking quietly and seriously, "At lunchtime we'll hover around the office corridor and set off the fire alarm. Then when everyone's outside, I'll go into the head's office and look in the filing cabinet marked, 'Staff'. I've seen it before when I had a meeting with the head and my mum and dad about Extra English classes."

"You're very observant, Ant," said Hal, "I can't say I ever noticed it."

"Well, it was a very boring meeting, so I switched off and catalogued all the furniture in my head."

"Why on earth did you do that?" asked Hal.

"Because I was embarrassed at everyone talking about my problems and I didn't want to listen. It was a bit like a game for me."

"But, Ant," said Hal hesitantly, "I'm not going into the office. I'm bound to get caught."

"No, I know that. I don't want you to come in. I need you on look-out duty."

"Look-out duty! What do you mean by that!" exclaimed Hal looking scared.

"Shhh – quiet," hissed Ant, "Someone will hear you. All you have to do is stand on the corner by the offices and if you see someone, give me a warning."

"A warning?"

"Yes, but I'm not sure how. Maybe you could clap your hands or cough loudly. Yes, that's it, cough loudly and then if anyone says anything, you can just keep on like you're having a coughing fit and they'll pat you on the back to help you."

"Help me? They're more likely to think I set the alarm off."

"No, they won't. You could say it's the smoke making you cough."

Hal looked at Ant with a sigh, "There will be no smoke, Ant. We're setting off the alarm. There *is* no fire." He paused and then continued, "All right, I'll be your lookout but if anyone asks me about the fire alarm, I will deny everything."

Ant grinned, "Of course. So will I."

Chapter 7 Ant sets off an alarm

Day 4 Friday lunchtime

Ant and Hal lurked around near the offices until there was no one about. There was a corner in the corridor which led to a storeroom and they stood there, out of sight of anyone coming out of the offices. Ant had already located the nearest fire alarm.

"Right," he whispered to Hal, "I'm going to set off the alarm. I'll come back here until the head and his secretary have gone and then I'll go to his office."

Hal nodded fearfully as Ant went up to the fire alarm.

Ant lifted the little hammer, holding his breath and closing his eyes, he broke the glass. Next, he opened his eyes and pressed the alarm button. The noise was so loud that he nearly jumped out of his skin.

He dashed back to Hal and waited. They did not have to wait long! Out came the head and his secretary from their adjoining offices, with the secretary clutching the 'Visitors' Book' under her arm.

"OK," said Ant, loudly this time, as the alarm was making such a din, "I'm off now. Remember to cough loudly if anyone comes back."

Ant rushed into the head's office and went to the filing cabinet marked 'Staff'.

Suddenly, he panicked thinking it might be locked, but luck was with him for once and the tray marked 'A – M' opened easily when he pulled it.

He looked for the 'B's and found 'BROWNLEES Michael' quite quickly. He reached for the file; ready to jam it in his school bag. Suddenly he thought that that the head would miss the file and alert Mr. Brownlees. He pulled the file out, marking the place it had come from with an exercise book from his bag. Holding his breath again, he looked at the single page of paper in the file. He spotted 'temporary caretaker' and the last employer was 'Springwater School'. He noticed his address was High Street and the number

Ant shoved the file back in the

filing cabinet.

was '12 a' (Ant's age and 'A' for Anthony, so he wouldn't forget that).

He shoved the file back – remembering at the last moment to grab his exercise book. Then he heard loud coughing. Ant peeped out of the door and could see that Hal was being patted on the back by Mrs. Walker, the deputy head and then she moved him swiftly down the corridor to the exit. Hal ran out of the office and headed for the other exit to the playground, which was down the corridor where the storeroom was located. He emerged outside to see all the classes lined up across the far side of the playground. He rushed over to his form's assembly point and his form teacher, Miss Parker, cried out in relief, "Anthony

Collins!   At last! Have you seen Harold Masters?"

'He's there Miss, with Mrs. Walker,' he said pointing across the playground to where Hal was still coughing and being led over to them by Mrs. Walker.

"Oh no,' called Miss Parker to Mrs Walker, 'Is it smoke inhalation?"

"No, I don't think so, there was no smell of smoke. He's OK now."

Ant heard a snigger behind him from Bazza Parsons, "Trust *Velcro* boy and Scaredy Cat to be late."

Ant could hear Bazza's mates laughing unpleasantly and thought smugly to himself,

"They wouldn't laugh if they knew what I'd been up to."

Ant was a bit shocked to see that a fire engine had turned up, but relieved when Miss Parker said, "It's a false alarm. You can all go back to your classes now."

Later he caught up with Hal and told him what he had found out.

"Let's go over to Springwater School tomorrow afternoon. I know where it is. I've been there before to an athletics match which my sister, Laura, was in last year. It's not far, we can cycle there in about half an hour and there's a playground next to it where we might be able to have a chat with one of the pupils."

Chapter 8 Ant goes to Springwater

Day 5 Saturday afternoon

On Saturday afternoon Ant and Hal met up with their bikes, ready to cycle to Springwater.

The route to Springwater took them along the coastal road which had a cycle path next to it. Even though it was late September, it was still warm and the sun made the sea sparkle. When they got to the top of the hill out of Meadowfield, they stopped for a rest. They could see the small town of Springwater spread out below them.

"Right," said Ant, "It's all downhill from here!"

They got back on their bikes and freewheeled down the hill as fast as they dared.

When they got to the school, there were a couple of cars in the car park but the school looked almost deserted.

"Just the cleaners and maybe the head," guessed Hal.

Ant nodded, "We won't get much from them, us being kids. Let's go to the playground – it's just over there."

Ant waved generally in the left hand direction past the school.

They got back on their bikes, pedalled past the school and dismounted before going through the playground gate. It looked nearly empty. There were some little children with their mums in the small playground with swings and roundabouts, just ahead of them. Over to the right was a skateboarding area and they could see a solitary figure gliding down a slope.

"Let's go over there," said Ant, "We could ask that boy about Mr. Brownlees."

They wheeled their bikes over to the skateboarding area, sat down on the grass beside it and pretended to chat, whilst surreptitiously watching the boy on the skateboard for a few minutes. He was obviously *not* a skilled skateboarder. He was trudging up the same slope each time carrying his skateboard, then coming down and trying to go up the opposite slope. But every time he nearly reached the top; he slid back down, stepped off and sometimes fell over. He kept trying and Ant noticed that he was getting higher up the second slope each time. It reminded him of the time he had been skateboarding and had the same problems.

Eventually, the boy reached the top of the slope, jumped off his skateboard and shouted, "Yes!" whilst punching the air.

Ant and Hal, both stood up and clapped loudly. The boy suddenly saw them. He had been so wrapped up in what he was doing that he hadn't noticed them. His face fell and he looked at them anxiously, in case they were mocking him, but then saw their

Ant and Hal clapped loudly.

friendly smiles and relaxed.

"Well done!" said Hal.

"Yes," agreed Ant, "You did really well. I've never been any good at skateboarding and couldn't have done that. I'm Ant and this is Hal by the way. Would you like a sweet?"

Ant pulled a bag of sweets out of his pocket offering it to the boy and Hal.

"Thanks, I'm Jamie. Are you from round here?"

"No, we're from Meadowfield. We've just come out for a bike ride," said Ant.

"We were just wondering, do you know Mr. Brownlees? He's the new caretaker at our school. Wasn't he here last term?"

"Yes, that's right. Our usual caretaker, Mr. Marston, was off sick for ages so he came as a temporary caretaker – from about last Christmas, I think."

"What was he like?" asked Hal, "Was he friendly?"

"Well, I wouldn't exactly say that," said Jamie, "He didn't have much to do with us, you know the pupils. He seemed really serious and didn't talk much to anyone. He was only really friendly with Mr. Potts who used to work here."

"Mr Potts?" Ant said excitedly, "He teaches 'History' at our school."

"Yes, that's right," agreed Jamie, "He used to teach here when I was in Year 7, I'm in Year 9 now, so he must have left well over a year ago. I only know they're friends because we live next to the harbour and I see them going fishing together at least twice a week. Well, I *used* to, up to last summer. I've not seen them lately."

"Fishing? That's interesting," reflected Ant, "What sort of boat did they have?"

"Well just a small sort of dinghy with an outboard motor – not a speedboat or anything like that."

They chatted to their new friend for a bit longer about people they knew at their schools and suddenly Hal looked at his watch and gave a start.

"Ant, we'd better go. It's nearly half past five and it'll take us at least half an hour to get home. My mum will be mad if I'm late for tea and we usually have it at six."

"Yeah, we'd better go," he nodded to Jamie, "Cheers, Jamie. I expect we'll bump into each other again. Keep up the skateboarding."

Jamie grinned, "Thanks for the sweets. Hope you get back in time, Hal."

They waved goodbye and set off back up the long hill towards Meadowfield.

As they cycled up the hill, Ant kept thinking about Mr. Potts. He was fine as a teacher, not one of his favourites, but OK. Ant remembered that Mr. Potts always got more excited when he was telling them about things like the Mary Rose, the Tudor ship that had been found under the sea, and smugglers in the past. Maybe, just maybe, he was a treasure hunter. It was just possible.

Chapter 9 Ant is worried

Day 7 Monday morning

On Monday Ant and Hal got a terrible shock.

At registration, Miss Parker announced, "Today, there will be an extra assembly at 11 o'clock this morning. Following the false fire alarm yesterday, Fire Officer Taylor is coming to talk to all pupils and staff."

Ant gulped, "*All* pupils and staff," he thought, "That never happens unless someone dies or it's an Awards Day."

The rest of the class were jubilant, "Great," said Maisie Woods, "No geography today!"

"That's quite enough," said Miss Parker, "This assembly is a very serious business. Someone started a false alarm and that is a punishable offence."

"Punishable offence?" Ant thought, "Does that mean I've broken the law? Will I go to prison?"

Ant found himself sweating and his heart pounding. Then the whole form stood up, picked up their school bags and left the room to go to the first lesson, science. Ant looked around and grabbed his school bag and followed them. Miss Parker looked at him strangely, "Is something the matter, Anthony, you look very pale."

"No, Miss, I've just got a bit of a headache. I'll be OK," he muttered.

"Well don't forget you can go to the school nurse if you're not well."

"OK, Miss," Ant said over his shoulder as he went out the door.

After break, they all trooped to the school hall and lined up class by class.

The head introduced Fire Office Taylor, who started to tell them how serious false alarms were and how the Fire Brigade could be late attending a real fire if they had to go to false alarms.

Ant felt himself shrink inside his body. His head pounded and he stopped hearing what

The Fire Officer told them not
to set off false alarms.

was being said. He closed his eyes and held his breath. He could hear the blood singing in his ears. Was this what they called a panic attack? He would have to calm himself down because, if he fainted, everyone would guess it was him. Then he realised everyone was shuffling off out of the hall and he opened his eyes expecting the head and Fire Officer to be looking at him accusingly. But they were shaking hands seriously and then walked off the stage at the front of the hall. No one seemed interested in him at all. Ant breathed a sigh of relief and headed off after the rest of his class.

He caught up with Hal who turned to him and said quietly, in case anyone heard,

"Were you scared, Ant, when the Fire Officer told us about how bad it was to set off hoax fire alarms? And, how you could be reported to the police?"

"No," said Ant casually, crossing his fingers behind his back, "I was fine. No probs."

Chapter 10   Ant overhears an important conversation

Day 7 Monday afternoon

That afternoon, it was P.E. again, which was always dreaded by Ant and Hal. On this occasion they were in the gym. They managed to get in the same group and stay out of the way of Macca and Bazza, so consequently it was not too bad. The other boys in their group were quiet and concentrating on their own skills and didn't look to see how Ant and Hal were getting on. Afterwards, the two friends, last as usual, wandered out of the changing rooms which led them past the building where the caretaker's office was located. Out of the corner of his eye Ant spotted Mr Brownlees deep in conversation with a teacher. It was Mr. Potts. He grabbed Hal and pulled him behind the dustbins so that they would not be seen. The two boys squatted out of sight. The men were coming their way whispering to each other. The boys felt like their ears were out on stalks trying to listen.

"Tonight ...... at the quay ...... clear skies ...... half moon," heard Ant.

The two men opened the door and went down the steps to the caretakers' room, still talking intently to each other and looking around furtively.

"Tonight, at the quay," whispered Mr. Potts.

"Did you hear that?" hissed Ant excitedly to Hal.

"Well, I heard the bit about the moon and clear skies," said Hal.

"And Mr. Potts said 'Tonight' and mentioned the quay," added Ant.

"Well, Jamie did say they go fishing together, so that's probably what it will be," answered Hal.

"But at night?" questioned Ant, "Do people go fishing in little boats at night? I know the proper fishermen do; in the trawlers out of the harbour at Springwater. But do the amateur line-fishermen go out at night?"

"I expect so. I know people go fishing overnight by the canal," added Hal with authority, "My uncle does, and he has a special shelter like a tent."

Ant pondered this for a minute and then his mind jumped to another idea.

"Hal, I've been thinking about skateboarding since we saw Jamie. I think I'll have another go and see if I can do a turn at the top of the slope. Let's go to the park near here after school. Will you come?"

"OK, Ant. I'll come but I'm not skateboarding. Last time I did it, I skinned both my knees and it really hurt."

"You should wear knee and elbow pads. It doesn't matter, you come and keep an eye open whilst I have a go, so we don't bump into any of those bullies, like Bazza and Macca. I'll go home and get my gear and meet you there at 4 o'clock."

Ant glanced at his watch. "Oh, no. We'd better hurry or we'll be late for maths."

The two boys scurried off and just got to the classroom at the last minute.

Chapter 11   Ant comes a cropper

Day 7   Later on Monday afternoon

Ant rushed home after school, grabbed his skateboard and rammed his knee and elbow pads into a carrier bag with his helmet. He raced over to the park to meet up with Hal.

When he got there, he found that there was no one else in the skatepark.   He breathed a sigh of relief and strapped on his pads and helmet.   He tucked his skateboard under his arm and walked up the lowest slope. He put his board down at the top, took a deep breath and balanced on it - that was OK.   Then bending his knees slightly, Ant pushed off tentatively with his back foot and before he knew it, he was gaining speed going down the slope. He reached the bottom and starting wobbling but managed to gain his balance and started up the opposite slope. Unfortunately, he did not have enough speed and soon rolled backwards. Ant jumped off and heard someone clapping. He whipped his head round and was relieved to see that it was Hal grinning all over his face.

"Hey, Ant, you did it and you didn't fall off!' he called encouragingly.

"I know," said Ant, "But even Jamie managed to get to the top of the other slope."

"How many goes have you had?" asked Hal.

"Just that one."

"Well, there you are, you haven't skateboarded for ages. You told me that earlier. Have another go."

Ant nodded, picked up his board and trotted up the slope. He put his board down, took his balance and pushed off again more strongly. This time there were no wobbles and he travelled all the way up to the top of the other slope, jumped off his board and cheered.

"I'm trying the higher slope this time!" he shouted to Hal.

"Be careful, Ant," warned Hal.

Ant stood on top of the higher slope, balanced on his board and kicked off strongly. Down he went like the wind, there was no stopping him. He went charging up the other slope and when he got to the top, he jumped off and cheered even louder.

"This time I'm going down and up, then changing direction at the top and down again!" he called to Hal.

Hal looked concerned.

With increasing confidence, Ant pushed off even faster and careered down the slope. He whizzed up the opposite slope and at the top executed a fast turn, but, unfortunately it did not work out properly. He found himself going very quickly down the slope whilst wobbling wildly. Then, he was flying through the air, as his board

Ant found himself flying through the air.

carried on in front of him. He landed awkwardly on the slope, banging his head as he fell. His helmet landed on the ground beside him.

Hal raced over to him and was horrified to find that he was unconscious.

"OMG, Ant. Wake up! You're not dead, are you?" he wailed loudly.

A lady came running over from the playpark, dragging her little girl by the hand and looked at Ant.

"It's all right," she said to Hal," He's still alive but he's banged his head. He obviously didn't put his helmet on properly. See the strap wasn't fastened correctly."

Hal nodded, gulping back his tears, "But will he be all right?"

"I should think so," she said reassuringly, "I'm a nurse."

She put Ant into the recovery position, and he was now making groaning noises.

"We had better call an ambulance though, just to make sure. He might have concussion."

She took her mobile out of her pocket and dialled "999".

Soon the ambulance arrived and took Ant off to hospital. The paramedics asked him for his telephone number, but he was too dazed to say.

"I can help," said Hal, "I'll go and tell his mum to go to the hospital. They only live round the corner from here."

He set off feeling very worried that he was in for a telling off for letting Ant go skateboarding. It wasn't really Hal's fault as Ant had decided to go without consulting him, but Hal always worried that anything that went wrong was his fault and that he would get in trouble.

When he got to Ant's house and knocked the door, his knees were shaking.

'Hello, Hal, did you want to see Anthony?" asked Ant's mum, "I'm not sure where he is. I thought he went to meet up with you."

Hal explained about the accident and Ant's mum went white and gasped, "He banged his head … an ambulance … hospital. I must go now."

She ran into the house, grabbed her car keys, shut the door and raced over to the car. Hal stood on the doorstep as she sped away. He thought he had better go home and tell his own mum what had happened. Hope she was OK with him!

Chapter 12 Ant spots something suspicious

Day 7 Later on Monday

Ant opened his eyes and saw bright lights which dazzled him. He seemed to be in something that was moving and he could hear people talking quietly. His eyes focussed and he looked up to see a man looking down at him.

"Where am I?" he muttered faintly.

"It's OK, lad. You're in an ambulance. You banged your head at the skatepark. We're just going to the hospital to have you checked over. Just relax."

Ant was feeling a bit sick, then it came back to him what had happened. He went cold. Who had seen him fall? Hopefully only Hal.

"Hal," he said, "My friend, where is he?"

"He went to get your mum," said the ambulance man, "I expect she'll be at the hospital soon. We're just pulling into A&E now. Someone will take a look at you and I expect your mum will be here soon."

Ant groaned. What would his mum say when she found he had been skateboarding? She always worried about things like that. He hadn't told her where he was going, only that he was meeting Hal.

After he had had his head examined, his mum came into the room.

"Oh, Anthony," she said, "Why weren't you more careful. They said you hadn't put you helmet on properly."

"Sorry, Mum. I didn't realise. Can we go home now?"

"No, Anthony, I'm afraid not. They think you might be concussed and they want to keep an eye on you for a few hours."

Ant groaned.

"Look Ant, they are going to take you to a ward. I'll come with you and settle you in. Then I've got to go back and get Laura and Dad's tea. I'll come back in a couple of hours and hopefully they'll let you come home then."

Ant gradually found that he was feeling better although the bump on his head was hurting quite a lot.

They gave him a cheese sandwich and some water; then he lay there hoping that his mum would come back soon. There was no TV in the ward, so he was really bored. He kept thinking about Mr. Brownlees and what was really going on with the treasure in his office.

When Mum came, she had a chat with the ward sister and they agreed that Ant could go home but not go to school tomorrow.

Ant and his mum got in the car and started off towards their house. They passed the school on the way and were stopped by traffic lights near the side entrance. Ant glanced out the window and saw Mr. Brownlees going through the side gate with a large bulky bag. What was he up to?

What was Mr. Brownlees up to?

Chapter 13   Ant finds more treasure

Day 9   Wednesday morning

Ant couldn't wait to get to school the next day to tell Hal what he had seen, but unfortunately his mum made him stay home and rest, so he did not get to school until Wednesday.   Ant told Hal, "I'm definitely going to find out what Mr. Brownlees was carrying into school on Monday night.   When we saw him it was nearly 10 o'clock?   He looked really sneaky, like he didn't want anyone to see him."

    "But, Ant, he might catch you," protested Hal.

"No," he said, "It's Wednesday and like last week, he'll go and see the head at 1 o'clock."

After lunch Ant hid himself round the corner of the building where Mr. Brownlees' office was. He peeped round surreptitiously when he heard the door open. It was Mr. Brownlees heading across to the main school building. Ant was relieved to see that he had his blue folder tucked under his arm this time.

When he was out of sight, Ant slipped through the door and down the stairs. He headed for the workbench. There was the big plastic box with the clip-on lid and on top of it was the bag he had seen Mr.

Brownlees carrying into school on Monday evening.

He examined the bag; it was like a sailor's duffel bag with string threaded through the top and looped through a metal clip at the bottom. He eased the top open carefully and couldn't believe his eyes – more treasure – shining necklaces, brooches with big jewels mounted in them, golden drinking cups, silver candlesticks and more!

"Wow! This looks like pirate treasure!" Ant said excitedly to himself. He grabbed a brooch to show Hal and shoved it in his blazer pocket. He tied up the bag again and

"Wow! This looks like pirate treasure!"

left it on top of the big box. He crept up the steps and peeped out of the door. No sign of anyone this time. Ant breathed a sigh of relief and walked back to school in the opposite direction to the one which Mr. Brownlees had taken. He didn't want to bump into the caretaker if he finished his meeting with the head early.

When he got back to the main building, he looked in the playground for Hal where they had planned to meet, near the door to the dining hall. Hal was standing there looking anxious and gave a big sigh of relief when he saw Ant.

"Hal, I've got something to show you, but not here, let's go where no one can see us."

The two boys headed for the back of the bike sheds and Hal was glad to see there was no one there.

"Look, Hal," he took the brooch out of his blazer pocket and held it up. It caught the rays of the sun and shone as if it was lit up. A large, dark green stone was cut into a shape with six edges and round the stone were smaller, glittery white stones.

"Ant, I reckon it's an emerald and those are diamonds," said Hal in awe, "It must be worth a lot of money. You'd better put it back or you could get arrested for stealing."

"No one knows I took it. I'm not going to keep it for myself. I'm keeping it as evidence. Mr. Brownlees must be up to something."

"But you don't really know, Ant. Say if it belongs to him – and the ring you took last time. He could report it to the head and then he'd get the police involved. Then we'd get searched!"

'I'll take it home and hide it with the ring. It's in my bedroom in my special box with my *Pokeman* cards. No one's going to find it there. Even my mum, when she tidies up, isn't interested in *Pokeman* cards."

Hal sighed, "Well, it's your funeral."

Ant groaned; he really didn't think that was a helpful thing for Hal to say.

Chapter 14   Ant hears something interesting

Day 10 Thursday afternoon

The next day after school, Ant's mum asked him to cycle down to the High Street and pick up some fish she had ordered at the fishmongers for their evening meal.

"Don't dilly dally, Ant. The fish shop closes at 5.30. You need to go straight there, or we won't have anything for our tea."

"No problem!" called Ant over his shoulder as he cycled off.

Ant remembered that when he had looked at the file in the head's office, he had seen that Mr. Brownlees lived in the

High Street at number 12a. He thought that before he collected the fish, he would just have a look and see exactly where Mr. Brownlees lived. He noticed that some of the even numbers were on the right-hand side of the street, but they were not all there. Quite often the shops had no numbers on them at all. He could see number 4 which was an ordinary little house. He guessed that the numbers went up from there as he had only just reached the High Street. He counted, "4, 6, 8, 10, 12."

Number 12 was a hairdresser's shop, that was odd. He cycled up to it and saw that there was a door next to the main door into the hairdresser's. It had number '12a' on it.

"Mr. Brownlees must live in a flat upstairs, above the hairdresser's," thought Ant to himself.

Ant knew that there was a little road at the back of the High Street, a service road, he thought it was called. It was so that people could get to the back of the shops, flats and houses and offload things or drive into their garages or parking spaces. He headed back down the High Street and turned left at the end and then left again into the service road.

He dropped his speed and carefully cycled up the back road counting "2, 4, 6, 8, 10, 12."

He stopped at number 12, there was a small gate leading into a back yard with steps up to the flat. Then he noticed to his amazement that two people were standing in the back yard talking - Mr. Potts and Mr. Brownlees! He quickly backtracked and leant his bike up outside number 8. Then he hunched down and sidled forward until he was near the gate. He strained to hear what they were saying, "A couple more journeys and we're done. Tonight ...... 7 o'clock ...... the jetty."

He suddenly remembered, "The fish!" and pedalled off at speed, back down the service road and up the High Street towards the fishmongers.

"Tonight …… 7 o'clock …… the jetty."

The fishmonger, Mr. Cummings, was just locking his door.

"Ah, Anthony," he said, "I was just about to give your mother a ring. She said she wanted the plaice for tonight."

"Oh, no, you didn't call her, did you?" asked Ant in a flap.

"No," said Mr. Cummings with emphasis, "I said, I was just about to."

Mr. Cummings went back into the shop and returned with the fish wrapped in white paper.

"Thanks, Mr. Cummings, I'll go back as fast as I can.!

"Yes, you had better hurry. I wouldn't want to be in your shoes if your mother doesn't get the fish in time to cook it."

"Bye!" called Ant, peddling quickly back down the High Street.

Whilst Mum was cooking the fish, Ant called Hal on the phone and told him what he had heard.

"They'll be there at 7 o'clock," he said, "Will you come with me and watch them."

"Ant, I'm not sure if Mum will let me come," said Hal.

"Tell her that you're coming round to my house to do homework," said Ant.

"Yes, she'll probably agree to that," answered Hal.

"Great, see you at the quay at 7. Meet me at the back of the fish and chip shop. They won't see us there."

Ant suddenly thought that it might be a good idea to take some binoculars with him. He knew his dad had some at the top of his wardrobe. He sneaked upstairs whilst the rest of the family were watching T.V. He put the binoculars in his rucksack and headed downstairs.

"Just going round to Hal's to do some homework!" he called as he left the house, as quickly as possible, before anyone could stop him.

Ant headed to the back of the fish and chip shop and found that Hal was already there.

"Good man, Hal," he said, giving him a 'high five'.

Chapter 15 Ant keeps a look-out

Day 10   Thursday evening

Ant and Hal peeped round the corner of the fish and chip shop.   After about five minutes, they saw the two men walk up carrying a step ladder, a big torch and a large empty sack.   The men headed down the quay and put the items in a dinghy with an outboard motor.   They jumped in, started up the motor and headed off across the bay.

The boys emerged from behind the fish and chip shop and walked down to edge of the quay.

"Why have they got a ladder?" asked Hal, "It doesn't make sense."

The light was getting dim, but they could see the boat go round close to the coast. Ant knew the coastline from his time in the Sea Scouts. He followed them with his binoculars. It was getting towards twilight, but he could still see where they were going. They were heading for Gull Cove where the Sea Scouts had sailed to once. It was only accessible by boat and had high cliffs and rocky outcrops surrounding it. They had got there at low water, pulled their dinghies up on the beach and then had a picnic and barbecue. Their leader had come in a safety boat in case any of the dinghies got into trouble. He had brought all the picnic stuff with him. It was great but they were told that they had to leave

Ant watched the men through his binoculars.

before the tide got too high. Their leader told them that sometimes when it was a spring tide, the sea came right up to the cliffs. Ant had explored the beach whilst they were there and had noticed that there was a cave or opening in the cliff above the beach. Ant guessed that that was where Mr. Brownlees and Mr. Potts's stash must be. He explained to Hal that they probably had the ladder to climb up to the cave.

Hal said, "Anyway, Ant, even if they have found treasure in that cave, it's probably 'finders keepers' and so they can keep it all."

"I'm not sure," Ant said seriously, "I'm remember that one of our Sea Scout leaders told us that anything like that belonged to the Crown." Ant recalled now that it was when they were sitting on the beach having their picnic; one of boys had joked about buried treasure and that he should have brought a metal detector.

Hal looked puzzled, "What's 'the Crown'?"

Ant nodded knowledgeably, "It means that it belongs to the Queen."

"What, the Queen of England?"

Ant nodded again.

"Wow!" exclaimed Hal, "She must be really rich!"

"Yes, that's right," said Ant, "Look Hal, we'd better go now, it's nearly dark."

As the boys hurried back home, Ant explained his plan to Hal.

"I'm going to investigate on Saturday, during daylight. I'll borrow Mr. Gimble's rowing boat. He showed me where it's tied up once, next to the slipway. I want to check the tides first so I get there around low water and then I can get up to the cave from the beach."

"But Ant, you said that the cave was high up. You won't be able to climb up there?"

"You're right, I'd better take a step ladder with me, like they did - and a torch."

"How are you going to smuggle a step ladder out of the house without your mum and dad seeing?" asked Hal.

Ant frowned, that was a fair point, "It'll have to be when they go to the big supermarket out at Soubury. They always go there on Saturday. I just hope that it fits in with the tide times. I'll balance the ladder on my bike and wheel it down."

"I hope nobody from school sees you!" Hal said with a grin.

"I'll work everything out and tell you when I'm going because I need you to be my look-out again."

"Wha-a-t, I hate boats and going on the water! I can't swim," protested Hal.

"No, I mean on the quay. I want you to be my back-up person and if I don't come back in a couple of hours, you can let someone know," explained Ant.

"Oh, all right then," said Hal doubtfully.

"Good man!" said Ant cheerfully, slapping him on the back.

Chapter 16 Ant looks at the tide tables

Day 11 Friday afternoon

On Friday, after school, Ant decided to plan for his adventure the next day. He walked down to the newsagent and bought a tide table booklet. Then he took it to his bedroom and tried to make sense of it.

On the cover it said: 'Tide Tables for Springwater'. He knitted his eyebrows, 'Springwater', did it make any difference that they were in Meadowfield? He supposed that they put 'Springwater' on it because there was a big harbour there and the Lifeboat Station, whereas at Meadowfield there was just a little quay and a slipway.

"And," he thought to himself, "The cave is about halfway between the two. Anyway, it's probably OK because they sell these tide tables in Meadowfield."

Ant opened the booklet and scanned the first page. He frowned, he knew that his reading and maths were not great, but this was like a code. At the top of the page was the month, so he leafed through until he got to September. The page was divided into little blocks which were in four columns and 8 rows. He realised that each block was for a different date as there was a bigger number at the top of each block in bold print. He scanned down the columns until he found tomorrow's date. Next to the date were eight numbers, arranged in two columns.

Ant sighed, "I wish that I paid more attention when they talked about Tide Tables in Sea Scouts."

At the time it had just seemed so complicated that he switched off, gazed out of the window of their club hut and watched the seagulls.

The chart read:

0213	1.9
0829	0.4
1433	1.8
2047	0.3

"What can it mean?" thought Ant, "Maybe the first column gives the times of high water. If they are times, why haven't they got a dot or something between them."

Ant scratched his head; he knew for certain that there were only two high tides each day. He knew that from living by the sea and watching the water go in and out. Why were there four times? He looked at the second column, maybe they were the heights of the tides?

"Yes," he said to himself, "I'm right – two small numbers and two bigger numbers. That must mean that low water is at ...... 8.29 and 20.47. That's about half past 8 in the morning and quarter to nine at night.

I'll have to go in the morning. It's a bit early but that's what I'll have to do."

He thought about the heights of the tide, "1.8 doesn't sound too much but that's at high tide, I'm going at low tide and that's 0.4. Does that mean the beach will be covered in water?"

Ant shook his head; his Sea Scout leader had told them that the beach only got covered in water at really high tides. The reading must be for the harbour at Springwater.

"So, it should be all right for me to go a bit later in the morning, about 11 when Mum and Dad go to the supermarket. As long as I'm back before half past two."

Ant put the Tide Table away in his drawer and went downstairs to phone Hal.

"Hi Hal," he said, "It's all sorted, meet me at the quay at 10.30."

"OK, Ant, will do," he paused, "But say if Mr. Potts and Mr. Brownlees decide to go the same time as you?"

"No, I don't think they will. It would look suspicious if they got back to the quay in the middle of the day on Saturday with all their stuff. Anyway, you bring your mobile with you and I'll bring mine then you can phone me if you see them set off and I'll come straight back."

"Righty-ho, see you tomorrow," said Hal.

"10.30 sharp, Hal," reminded Ant, "Bye."

Chapter 17   Ant sets off

Day 12 Saturday morning.

The next day started like an ordinary day but it was about to become one of the most exciting days Ant had ever experienced.

Ant got up as usual, had his breakfast and made his bed. He felt so excited he just could not wait to go. He noticed that it was about half past 9.

He went downstairs and asked his mum, "Are you going shopping this morning, Mum?"

"Yes, as usual," she answered, "Anything you want me to get you especially?"

"No, it's OK, maybe you could get me some sweets. You know my favourites."

"Yes, I will," said Mum, "Dad and I will be leaving soon. We're giving Mrs. Tolley from next door a lift. Her car's off the road and she asked if she could come with us."

Ant went in the sitting room and pretended to watch Saturday morning TV, but he just kept going through his plans in his head.

Suddenly he thought, "The step ladder! Where is it?"

His heart started racing. He would try the shed.

Ant slipped out the back door to the shed and looked inside. He breathed a sigh of relief. There it was propped up against the wall.

He looked at his watch, it was 10 o'clock and Mum and Dad still hadn't left.

"Are you off then?" he asked his mum.

"Well, there's a problem with Mrs. Tolley. She just popped in and said she had to phone the garage about her car. Apparently, the garage is open on Saturday mornings and they want to talk to her about the repairs."

Ant groaned inwardly.

At last Mrs. Tolley arrived and left with Mum and Dad in the car at 10.25.

"Your lunch is in the fridge, Laura's gone round to Olivia's so she'll have lunch there," said Mum over her shoulder as she went out, "And don't forget to lock the door if you go out."

Ant breathed a sigh of relief that his sister Laura had gone out. There was no one to see him take the step ladder out. He texted Hal as quickly as he could, "Running late. Be there soon. A." Ant grabbed his mobile and the big torch, which hung up over the back door, on his way to the shed.

Ant carried the step ladder out. His bike was propped against the wall of the house. He wheeled it out through the side gate and then came back for the ladder. He shoved his mobile in his pocket and hooked the

torch on the handlebars. Ant balanced the
ladder on his bike. It was a bit wobbly but
if he put one hand on the handlebars and
the other on the ladder, he hoped he would
manage. He started off down the path and
then suddenly remembered that he had not
locked the house. He balanced the bike and
stepladder against the hedge round the
front garden and ran back to lock up.

Then he thought, with a start, what
about a life jacket? He never went out on
the water without a life jacket or buoyancy
aid. He ran upstairs and got the life jacket,
he always wore when he went sailing with
Dad, from the top of his wardrobe. He put
it on, fortunately, it was one of the
lightweight ones that inflated if you fell in

the water. Finally, he was ready to set off. He was hoping none of the neighbours were watching.

Ant found it took him much longer than the usual fifteen minutes to walk to the quay. The bike kept wobbling and he had to keep adjusting the position of the step ladder. When he eventually got there, he spotted Hal sitting on a bench, swinging his legs.

"At last!" said Hal, "You're really late. It's gone 11 o'clock."

"It'll be OK," said Ant, "High tide isn't until half past 2. If I'm not back by 2 o' clock, then you had better phone me and find out what's happening. Don't forget to phone me if you see Mr. Potts and Mr. Brownlees going out in their boat."

"Where's Mr. Gimble's boat?" asked Hal.

"Just down there by the slipway," he said pointing and wheeling his bike along the quay.

"Here, you look after my bike and I'll put the stepladder in the bottom of the boat."

Ant manoeuvred the stepladder in place and was relieved to see that Mr. Gimble had stored his oars under the seat. He pulled them out and put them in the rowlocks. Then he shouted to Hal, "I've left the torch on the bike, please can you pass it to me."

Hal carefully put the bike on the ground and passed Ant the torch. Then the two boys pushed the rowing boat down the slope; luckily the boat had little rollers on the underside which made it a bit easier to push. Hal held the boat by the rope at the front, until Ant had got in and then threw it to Ant and pushed the boat into the water.

"Good luck, Ant!" he shouted, wondering to himself what on Earth Ant was getting himself into. Ant had told him that he had rowed lots of times with his dad, but he was sure that Ant's dad would be furious if he knew that he had gone out on his own. What would happen if Ant got into trouble? He was his only look-out. He sat down on the bench with Ant's bike propped next to him, staring out to sea watching Ant and the rowing boat getting smaller and smaller as

he headed towards the cove.

Hal pushed the boat into the water.

Chapter 18 Ant finds the hoard

Day 12 Midday Saturday

Ant rowed steadily towards the cove, it was hard work, but he had the tide with him. It took him much longer than he had expected. As the rowing boat ground to a halt, he glanced at his watch and noticed that it was nearly half past 12. He got out and pulled the boat up onto the beach as far as it would go. He noticed that the beach looked smaller than when he had been there in the summer with the Sea Scouts. He stored the oars and his life jacket in the bottom of the boat. Then he tried to tie the rope to a rock, but it would not stay tied.

He then found a big boulder and put it on the rope to keep the boat from floating away.

Ant took the stepladder out and positioned it below the cave. He picked up the torch and looped it round his wrist. Carefully he climbed up the stepladder. When he got to the top, he still hadn't reached the cave and had to haul himself up the last few centimetres. In his effort to get on the rock ledge, his mobile slipped out of his pocket.

"I'll pick it up before I row back," thought Ant, "I don't fancy climbing back down and up again."

Ant climbed the stepladder to
get to the cave.

In fact, Ant could feel his heart beating with excitement. He had made it and was only a short distance from discovering the truth about the treasure.

Ant crouched on the rock ledge and looked into the cave. It was quite narrow and low. He could see that the rocky passageway led round a corner, winding inwards and upwards. Ant set off into the cave, switching his torch on, as it got darker the further he went. He had to crouch down as the roof of the passageway got lower and eventually ended up crawling on his hands and knees. He realised that there was now no daylight and his torch was absolutely essential.

It seemed like he had reached the end of the passage as he flashed his torch around. Then he saw it, an old wooden chest with metal hasps and bands round it. He opened the heavy lid and looked inside. It was definitely where the men had found the treasure but there was not a lot left - some goblets and plates. It was obvious that the men had left the bigger items for their last visit.

Ant started examining the items by torchlight. He took out a magnificent goblet, which shone like gold in the torchlight and had beautiful stones inset around the outside. He looked carefully and saw that they were red and green cut stones.

"Maybe rubies and emeralds and a gold cup," he said to himself in awe.

Then he took out one of the plates which also looked like gold. It looked like it had been made by hand and he could see silver patterns round the edge and a figure of a lady in the middle. Ant was absolutely enthralled by what was in the chest and took each piece out, one by one, to examine very carefully. He had seen some things in the local museum which looked a bit like one or two of them and remembered that they had been marked as '15th Century'.

Ant started wondering which ones he ought to take back with him as evidence and chose the first goblet and plate which he had spotted. He felt a bit miffed with himself that he had forgotten to bring a bag to put them in, so he would have to put them in the bottom of the rowing boat. Ant thought he had better check the time and was horrified to see that it was now gone half past one. He had no idea that it had taken him so long to get the boat on the beach, climb up the ladder into the cave and examine the treasure.

Ant picked up the goblet and plate and started crawling back down towards the entrance. He had not realised he had come so far. As he came round the last bend, he was relieved to see daylight and moved towards the entrance. He looked down to where the stepladder was and was amazed and startled to find that it was no longer there. The water had covered the beach and the waves were splashing against the cliff just below him. He found that he could lean over and nearly touch the water.

He looked up towards the horizon and could see Mr. Gimble's rowing boat floating out to sea. Obviously, the big boulder had not been heavy enough and the rope had come free. The stepladder and mobile phone were nowhere to be seen.

Ant did not know what to do. He thought, "It's up to Hal, now."

But Hal had been told to phone him at 2 o'clock and that was not for another half an hour. Also, if Mr. Potts and Mr. Brownlees were coming out to the cave, Hal was meant to phone him and Ant's phone was now under the water on the beach.

Chapter 19   Ant is trapped in the cave

Day 12   Saturday afternoon

Ant looked out from his ledge, it was now 2 o'clock and the water level was still rising. The waves were starting to splash over the edge of the ledge and seemed to be gathering in strength.

Ant moved back inside the cave to keep dry, taking the precious treasure with him.

Hopefully, realising that he wasn't answering his phone, Hal would now raise the alarm and at the very least phone his mum and dad. Then he thought, they will have to come and find me before water gets too high. Ant shivered, he was feeling cold and scared.

"What will I do if the water gets higher?" he asked himself. He had noticed that the treasure chest was on a ledge at the back of the cave. "It's probably been there for hundreds of years, so it's not really likely that the cave will flood back there. If the worse comes to the worst, I'll have to go and sit on the treasure chest on the ledge and wait until the tide goes out."

Ant felt better after working that out. Hopefully, someone would come and rescue him soon anyway.

Time passed slowly for Ant, as he listened to the waves splashing into the cave. Eventually he realised that the sound of the waves was getting less and he started moving back towards the entrance.

Then he realised that he could hear the sound of a boat's engine and that it was getting closer. He asked himself, "Is it someone coming to rescue me, or is it Mr. Potts and Mr. Brownlees coming for their final haul?"

In a panic, Ant scuttled further back into the cave wondering where he could hide himself if it was the two treasure hunters. He could now hear men's voices as the boat got closer.

Then he heard his name being called, "Anthony, Ant, are you there?"

He could not believe his ears; it was a voice he recognised. It was Mr. Gimble!

Ant crawled to the edge of the cave, taking his treasure with him. There was Mr. Gimble sitting in the RNLI rescue boat. It was the smaller one that he had seen on the harbour at Springwater.

The skipper called to him, "Anthony, move to the edge of the cave and Greg, here, will help you down."

"Can I give you these first," said Ant, indicating the goblet and the plate, "It's valuable treasure, evidence you see."

The lifeboat man called Greg reached up and passed the items down to Mr. Gimble for safe keeping. He then helped Ant to climb down into the boat whilst the skipper held it steady on the engine.

Ant crawled to the edge of the cave.

As they start moving slowly away from the cave, Ant spotted Mr. Gimble's boat floating in the bay.

"Mr. Gimble, there's your rowing boat. I'm so sorry. I borrowed it and now it's floated away with my life jacket in it," Ant said shamefacedly.

The skipper looked at Ant with a very serious face, "It's all right, Anthony, we'll go and pick up Mr. Gimble's rowing boat now. However, you have been a very foolish boy going out in a boat without an adult and not even telling your parents, from what I've heard. At least you remembered to wear a life jacket. Mr. Gimble tells me that you are in the Sea Scouts. What do you think your leader would say about you borrowing a boat without permission and going out without any supervision? And," he said in exasperation, "You couldn't have chosen a worse day for it, it's a full moon and a spring tide!"

Ant's face had gone bright red, he looked down and studied his wet feet. He knew the skipper was right on all counts. He should have known about the spring tide. He just looked at the tide charts for today and 1.8 didn't sound much.

Mr. Gimble patted him on his back, "What were you doing, Anthony? Why did you go out to the cave? And what are these?" He held up the goblet and the plate.

As they went to collect Mr. Gimble's rowing boat and tie it up to the RNLI boat, Ant explained what had happened and about Mr. Potts and Mr. Brownlees.

Mr. Gimble nodded his head as Ant finished, "I thought there was something strange about that plane ticket to Australia; I didn't even remember entering a competition. It looks like they wanted me out of the way. My friend, Mr. Coates, who works in the grounds at school wrote me a letter saying that he suspected something suspicious was going on around the caretaker's office. Lots of comings and goings from this new caretaker and one of the teachers.

"My friend often works at the weekends and evenings doing odd jobs, cutting the grass for example, so he sees things maybe other people don't see. He told me he'd seen them bringing sacks of things on to the premises and when they spotted him, they took off pretty sharpish.

"Anyway, I've had a couple of months out in Australia and saw my sister, who I hadn't seen for years, so that was good. I talked to her about Mr. Coate's letter and she agreed with me that I had better come back. I went to the airline ticket office and they agreed to change the date of my return ticket. So here I am!"

"But how are you *here*?" asked Ant, "How did you come to be with the RNLI boat?"

"Well, I got back from Australia this morning and was just unpacking my bags when I heard a big ruckus outside. There was your friend, Hal, running up to his nan's house in a terrible state, shouting out and banging on her door. She wasn't in. I knew that because I had seen her going out to the shops when I arrived. I'd had a chat with her about coming home from Australia early.

"I calmed Hal down and asked him what the matter was. He said you had gone out to Gull Cove in my rowing boat to look for treasure, which took me back a bit, I'll tell you! Then he told me that you weren't answering your mobile and that he had tried your mum and dad's, his parents' and his nan's number but no one had answered. He was also muttering about these men who might have caught you in the cave. Well, I sat him down in my kitchen and phoned 999, I reckoned that it must be serious. I spoke to the operator and told them I knew where this cave was, that Hal was talking about, because I used to go fishing round that way in Gull Bay. I also used to be an active RNLI man myself. I help out a bit now, at the Lifeboat Station showing visitors round at weekends," he added pausing for breath.

"It was agreed that Hal and I would go back to the quay and the inshore rib lifeboat would pick me up so that I could show them where the cave was and put you at ease, so to speak. They also had alerted the police, as there was talk of treasure hunters and Hal being scared you were in danger.

"Anyway, the RNLI boat picked me up and Hal spoke to the policeman and explained what had happened. The police are going to let your mum and dad know, so they'll probably be at the quay when we get back there."

Ant groaned inwardly, they were approaching the quay now and sure enough, he could see Hal, the policeman and his mum and dad watching as the boat got closer. "Oh no, "thought Ant, "I'm in for it now!"

Chapter 20   Ant helps the Police with their enquiries

Day 12 Saturday afternoon

The RNLI boat moored at the quay and Greg helped Mr. Gimble and Ant out.

As they got ready to leave, the skipper said, "Don't forget young Anthony, no more rowing out on your own! You're a very lucky lad to have escaped unharmed. You could have been trapped overnight or drowned. I will talk to your Sea Scout leader and let him know so he can have a word with you too."

Ant turned around as his mum came up to him and hugged him, "Oh, I'm so glad you're safe. What possessed you to go out on your own in a rowing boat? Surely you should know better from sailing with your Dad and the Sea Scouts!" There were tears in her eyes which she quickly wiped away with the back of her hand.

"Your mum's right, Anthony," joined in Dad with a frown, "You've been very foolish. P.C. Hobbs here wants to have a word with you as well."

Ant felt embarrassed and wished he could disappear. He knew they were right. He should have told his mum and dad about everything and left it to them to deal with. But would they have believed him? Would they have gone and spoken to the headmaster, who would have had a word with Mr. Potts and Mr. Brownlees? He was

160

sure the two men would have denied everything. It would have all been forgotten and the men would have escaped with the treasure.

P.C. Hobbs came up to him, "Look here, young man. I think you have been very unwise, but you've been told that already from what I've just heard. Your friend here, has been telling me what you two lads have been up to and Mr. Gimble has just given me these." He held up the plate and the goblet. "I think the museum will be *very* interested in them."

"I want you both to come to the station and we'll take a statement from you. I have

"I want you both to come to the police station."

rung your mum now, Hal, and she'll meet us at the station. Mr. and Mrs. Collins, please would one of you come too."

"I'll come," said Dad.

Mum nodded, "Yes, I will take your bike with me, as I had better get home before Laura gets back from her friend's."

Ant groaned inwardly as Mum headed off down the road, he expected that his big sister, Laura, would also have something critical to say about his adventure.

"What about Mr. Potts and Mr. Brownlees and the treasure?" asked Ant.

"Don't worry lad, I've alerted the station, we'll sort them out," said the policeman.

Ant looked anxiously at Hal, who was also looking very worried at the prospect of going to the Police Station to give a statement.

"Will we be arrested?" he asked tentatively.

P.C. Hobbs laughed, "Well, blow me down, lad. I shouldn't think so. More likely you'll get an award for getting all the treasure back to its rightful owner."

"Is it the Crown?" asked Ant, "Will the Queen get it all?"

"Well technically you're correct, but actually it will probably go to the local museum. We will report it all to the Coroner and he will decide."

"The Coroner!" exclaimed Hal, "I thought that was when people died or were - you know murdered." His voice dropped to a hush on the final word.

"Well, yes, but he also decides on 'Treasure Trove'. I suppose it's because the treasure was all from a long time ago and all the original owners are dead now."

"Cool," says Hal looking amazed.

"Well, I'm off now, officer," said Mr. Gimble, "Will you be needing a statement from me about this supposed prize of an air ticket to Australia?"

"I'm not sure, sir," said the policeman gravely, "It may be nothing to do with these two men, but if it is, we'll be in touch."

The four of them made off towards the Police Station in the High Street: Ant, Hal, Ant's dad and P.C. Hobbs. As they were walking along, Ant remembered with a start about the lost mobile phone and the stepladder.

"Um, Dad," he muttered, "I've got something else to tell you."

His dad's face looked serious, "Go on, Anthony, spit it out."

"My mobile phone fell in the water at Gull Cove and your step ladder was on the beach and disappeared," he blurted out.

"My stepladder, whatever did you need that for?"

"To climb into the cave," Ant said sheepishly.

"Oh, well," said Dad, "Worse things happen at sea, I suppose. I'll go out in my dinghy tomorrow at low tide to have a look on the beach. I have to say that it would be a miracle if your mobile works *even* if we find it."

"Oh, Dad, there's something else," said Ant with a frown.

"Whatever next!" exclaimed his father,

"I've got two things at home which I got from the caretaker's office. A ring and a brooch."

"Anthony, they don't belong to you, we had better tell P.C. Potts right away and bring them down to the Police Station as soon as possible."

"Evidence, Dad," Ant explained, "I kept them as evidence."

Chapter 21 What happened next?

Day 14 Monday morning

On Monday, Ant and Hal, returned to school to find Mr. Gimble back at his old job. Mr. Brownlees and Mr. Potts were nowhere to be seen. They had heard on the local news that two men had been arrested for finding 'Treasure Trove' and not reporting it. The men should have reported it within 14 days but had actually found it several months ago.

At registration, Miss Parker, looked up from marking who was present and said, "Anthony Collins and Harold Masters, you are to see the headmaster immediately after registration." She frowned and looked very serious.

The rest of the class erupted into comments and titters.

"What have they done, Miss?" asked Maisie Woods.

Bazza and Macca laughed and made faces at each other.

"That's enough, class, quiet down. End of registration," said Miss Parker with an air of finality, determined not to comment on Maisie's question.

Ant and Hal slipped out of the class as quickly as they could and made for the head's office. They knocked on the secretary's door.

"Mr. Barlow wants to see us, Miss," volunteered Hal nervously.

The secretary looked up from her computer and pointed at the two chairs outside the office.

"Just sit there, boys. Mr. Barlow will let you know when he's ready."

They both sat down, feeling sick in the pit of their stomachs.

After a couple of minutes, Mr. Barlow opened his door and said, "Anthony and Harold, in here."

Ant looked at him in amazement, he was smiling.

"Right boys take a seat," he said, "First of all I know that you have had a lot of criticism for borrowing Mr. Gimble's rowing boat, and also you, Ant, for rowing out to the cove. Which was very foolish and dangerous," he added more seriously, "However, I must tell you that you two have saved the reputation of the school and the treasure is no longer on school premises. It has been returned to its rightful place."

Ant and Hal breathed a collective sigh of relief.

"I must say, Harold, that your common sense on Saturday saved a difficult situation from getting worse and you may well have saved Anthony from a worse fate."

Harold blushed and smiled in embarrassment as Ant grinned and patted him on the back saying, "Thank you, Hal."

"As well you might, Anthony," nodded Mr. Barlow, "Right boys off to class now. For the time being, as this is a police matter, I would appreciate it if you kept what you know to yourselves."

The two boys nodded and retreated out of the door.

* * *

A few weeks later, when the two men's case came to court, it was reported on local television and radio, with pictures of some of the treasure they had found. It was apparent that the two men had found the cave and the hoard several months previously. They had decided to keep it and sell it for themselves. They sold a couple of pieces of jewellery at the beginning of the summer and made enough money out of that to buy a plane ticket for Mr. Gimble.

Mr. Brownlees' temporary job had finished at Springwater School and he was looking for another post. Mr. Potts had decided that it would be a good idea for him to take Mr. Gimble's job at Meadowfield because there was plenty of space to store things there. Meadowfield was also much quieter than Springwater and they would not be noticed as much, going in and out of the quay with sacks and bags of the treasure from the cave. They decided to send Mr. Gimble the airline ticket, pretending it was a prize from a competition. Mr. Potts wrote the letter and made it look convincing. Mr. Gimble took the bait and Mr. Potts told the headmaster that his friend Mr. Brownlees was looking for a job.

Mr. Gimble was very proud to go to court and give evidence of the scam. Ant and Hal did not have to appear in court but their statements were read out.

The next thing that happened was that the local paper rang up their parents and asked them if the boys could have their photo taken with the treasure hoard which had now been released to the local museum.

As they were about to have their photo taken, the museum curator, Mrs. Armstrong, came over and told them they were going to have a reward. She gave them a cheque for £5000 each. The boys were speechless. Ant had enough for a new mobile phone and a new bike and with plenty left to go in his savings.

* * *

The final surprise for the two boys did not happen until June, the following year. Every year the school had an Awards Ceremony attended by the whole school with guest speakers. All the school had to attend and Ant usually found it was really boring. He had no chance of winning an award for sport or what they called 'academic achievement'.

The guest speaker turned out to be Mrs. Armstrong from the museum who had brought several of the treasures with her to show the school. She explained how old they were, from about the 16th Century and how they were probably a pirate's hoard or maybe someone had hidden them there from a wrecked ship. Nobody would ever really know for sure. Some of the items were from Spain, so the ship might have been a Spanish galleon. At the end of her talk, she said, "I have two pupils to thank for finding this valuable treasure, Anthony Collins and Harold Masters. On behalf of the Meadowfield Museum, I have certificates of special service to be presented to these pupils. Please would you both come to the front."

Ant and Hal shuffled to the front, not knowing what to expect. They walked up the steps and shook hands with Mrs. Armstrong and the head, who was smiling broadly and said, "Well done, boys!"

Mrs. Armstong announced, "I have a very special person to present these certificates - Mr. Gimble."

Mr. Gimble stepped forward from the back of the stage with the certificates in his hand and presented them to the two boys whilst shaking their hands. The whole school clapped loudly, as everyone now knew the story, thanks to the local newspaper.

Ant and Hal walked back to where their class was sitting, clutching their certificates.

"Wow!" said Hal.

"Awesome!" uttered Ant.

Mr. Gimble presented Ant and
Hal with their certificates.

42498316R00105

Printed in Poland
by Amazon Fulfillment
Poland Sp. z o.o., Wrocław